CONTENTS

CHARACTERS

JOSH   MARS001

VOCABULARY

auction	nervous
costume	nonsense
impressed	pranks
inspecting	signature
mayor	surrounded

THE BOY WHO CRYED ALIENS!

BY
DANNY PEARSON
&
ABBY RYDER

Titles in Once Upon *Another* Time…

PRINCESS FROG-SNOGGER
BY TOMMY DONBAVAND & MARK PENMAN

LITTLE RED
BY BARRY HUTCHISON & MARK PEARCE

THE LEAGUE OF ENCHANTED HEROES
BY TIM COLLINS & JAMES LAWRENCE

THE BOY WHO CRIED ALIENS!
BY DANNY PEARSON & ABBY RYDER

GOLDIE LOCKED!
BY IAN MACDONALD & MARC ELLERBY

ED AND THE SHIRTMAKERS
BY ANDY SEED & RACHAEL SMITH

Badger Publishing Limited
Oldmedow Road,
Hardwick Industrial Estate,
King's Lynn PE30 4JJ

Telephone**: 01438 791037**
www.badgerlearning.co.uk

2 4 6 8 10 9 7 5 3 1

The Boy Who Cried Aliens!
ISBN 978-1-78464-530-4

Text © Danny Pearson 2016
Complete work © Badger Publishing Limited 2016

Publisher: Susan Ross
Senior Editor: Danny Pearson
Editorial Coordinator: Claire Morgan
Illustration: Abby Ryder
Designer: Fiona Grant

CHAPTER ONE
OPERATION SHED SCARE

There once was a boy named Josh who loved to play practical jokes on people.

He would spend hours planning pranks that would annoy his friends, family... everyone really.

He had already got into a lot of trouble for his most recent alien pranks but he found it all great fun.

Josh's mum and dad had invited people over for a BBQ.

The oldies were sitting in the shade talking about the good old days. The mums were eating cheese. The dads were standing around the BBQ eyeing up the meats and the kids were running around.

Everyone was having a great time. Everyone except Josh. He was bored.

"I need to liven this party up", Josh said to himself.

He ran upstairs to grab his latest costume.

He then quickly ran round the side of the house and hid his costume in the hedge beside the shed.

It was time for *Operation Shed Scare.*

Josh ran into the middle of the garden waving his arms. "Quick, everyone – I saw something in the shed!"

Everyone got up and made their way over to have a look.

While they were busy inspecting the shed, Josh quickly dived into the hedge to change into his costume.

With one giant leap, Josh jumped from the hedge, screaming at the top of his voice!

"*RAAAAAAAAAA!*"

The oldies fell backwards. The dads squeaked like mice and the mums picked up the nearest weapon.

Babies filled their nappies and the dog barked loudly.

Josh flipped off his mask and began to laugh.

"*HA HA HA!*"

CHAPTER TWO
KING OF THE WORLD

No one was impressed. Josh's mum and dad were very angry. They had already had complaints from his school, other parents and even the mayor about his alien pranks.

"What have we told you about your pranks? Get to your room NOW, Josh!"

Josh ran up the stairs and slammed his bedroom door shut.

BOOM!

"Everyone is so boring. If I ran the world things would be different... very different!"

A smile appeared on his face. "HA! I am king of the world. I can do whatever I want!"

He opened his laptop and pulled up his *We Sell Anything!* profile and decided to put something very large up for sale...

For sale: one planet called Earth – slightly used. Starting bid = 1p

WE SELL ANYTHING!
PLANET EARTH!!!

BUY NOW! 1P

POSTAGE: COLLECT ONLY
CONDITION: SLIGHTLY USED

ALI

Very early the next morning Josh was woken up by a ping from his computer.

Someone called **Mars001** had put in a bid of 10p for Planet Earth and they had won the auction. They had also left a message:

Dear Josh,
Thank you very much for Planet Earth. We will be over shortly to pick it up.
All the best,
Mars001

CHAPTER THREE

THE BOY WHO
SOLD THE WORLD

Who would be silly enough to put a bid on?
thought Josh.

Suddenly, there was a bright light at the window.
He slowly walked over and opened it.

A furry face stared right back at him.

"Hi", the little creature said with a smile. "We are
here to pick up Earth. Thank you very much. We just
need your signature please."

Josh turned white and ran from his bedroom and into his parents' room. "MUM! DAD! There is an alien outside my window!"

His mum and dad shot up and screamed at him. "Enough of this rubbish Josh, get back to your room NOW!"

Josh ran down the stairs screaming. He was being followed by the little aliens.

He tripped over the front door mat and rolled out into his street shouting at the top of his voice, "Somebody please help! ALIENS!"

One by one his neighbours looked out of their windows.

One of them shouted, "You again. Be quiet and go back to bed. It's too early for your nonsense!"

Josh was stood in the middle of the street surrounded by little aliens. They looked like they were ready for some heavy building work.

The aliens were moving in.

Neighbours hung out of their bedroom windows with their mouths wide open.

Josh looked at the aliens and then looked at the watching crowd of people.

With a nervous smile he shouted to the street, "See, I told you... ALIENS!"

STORY FACTS

This book is based on the story of *The Boy Who Cried Wolf.*

In that story, a boy, who looks after sheep in a field, keeps running down to his village crying out that a wolf is about. He is only joking and there is no wolf. After a while the villagers stop believing him and on the day when a wolf actually does appear no one bothers to help the boy. This leads to all the sheep being gobbled up!

I remember hearing this being read out at school. The lesson we were supposed to learn from the story is that you should not lie.

I thought it was a very strange story. A better lesson would be to say NO if anyone asked you to look after a flock of sheep on your own when you know there are wolves in the area!

So I updated the story and gave it an out-of-this-world twist.

QUESTIONS

Where had Josh played his alien pranks before? *(page 7)*

What happened after Josh had jumped out at the BBQ? *(page 14)*

How much did the user Mars001 buy Earth for? *(page 20)*

Where did Josh run first to ask for help from the aliens? *(page 24)*

What do you think the aliens plan to do with Earth?

MEET THE AUTHOR

Danny Pearson was very much a child of the 80s. He was brought up on a diet of unusual cartoons and movies involving things changing  into other things, or adventures set to cheap keyboard soundtracks. He has worked on hundreds of publications for teachers and students.

MEET THE ILLUSTRATOR

Abby Ryder is a cartoonist who loves comic books and video games.

Her greatest life ambition is to one day become best friends with a giant robot.